To the Keizers, Best Neighbors Ever,
and to
Makenna the Princess Warrior

Farrar Straus Giroux Books for Young Readers
An imprint of Macmillan Publishing Group, LLC
120 Broadway, New York, NY 10271

Text copyright © 2021 by Amy Young
Color separations by Bright Arts (H.K.) Ltd.
Printed in China by Toppan Leefung Printing Ltd.,
Dongguan City, Guangdong Province
Designed by Sharismar Rodriguez
First edition, 2021

1 3 5 7 9 10 8 6 4 2

mackids.com

Library of Congress Cataloging-in-Publication Data is available.

ISBN 978-0-374-31422-4

Our books may be purchased in bulk for promotional, educational, or business use.
Please contact your local bookseller or the Macmillan Corporate and Premium Sales Department
at (800) 221-7945 ext. 5442 or by email at MacmillanSpecialMarkets@macmillan.com.

A Unicorn Named SPARKLE and the Perfect Valentine

Amy Young

FARRAR STRAUS GIROUX

NEW YORK

"It's Valentine's Day, and there's a party!" said Lucy.
"I'm going to make cards for our friends. I will tell each
friend what I love about them."

She got busy.
"Don't worry. No one expects a valentine from a unicorn, so my cards can be from both of us."

There were a lot of things
Sparkle loved about Lucy.

He loved her curly black hair.

He loved her great big laugh.

He loved that she loved him best of all.

But how could he tell her all that? Maybe he could make a card and surprise her!

He took some paper and
paint and snuck off to
work in secret.

As a unicorn, Sparkle was great at a lot of things. He could make rainbows shoot out of his horn;

he could eat twenty cupcakes at a time and not get sick;

and he could poop glitter.

But he had never
made a card
before,

and he

didn't

know

how.

He cut a heart shape with his horn. It was harder than he thought. He kept trying until he got one that was okay.

He didn't know how to write, so to say that he loved Lucy's curly black hair, he made a hoofmark.

To say that he loved her great big laugh,
he made another hoofmark.

And to say that he loved her best of all, he made a third
hoofmark. He pressed so hard that it tore the paper.

The card was all done. It looked good to Sparkle.
But then Lucy said:

"Look, Sparkle. I wrote a poem for Shayla."

"I wrote poems for all our friends."

Sparkle realized that his valentine wasn't done
after all. It needed a poem.

He tried his best: He dipped his horn
in the paint and made a squiggly line on the card.

As he did that, he thought of this poem:

Sometimes I'm smelly
Sometimes I'm a pest
But I'll always love you
The best of the best!

There. Now his card was done!

"Sparkle!" called Lucy. "It's time to go
to the party! Come on!"

Put your Valentines HERE

Your

You matter!

LUCY

As soon as they got there,
Sparkle could see that all
the other cards were
much, much
fancier
than
his.

Next to the others, Sparkle's card looked messy and torn. It didn't have any glitter or lacy trim on it. The writing wasn't even real.

When he thought no one was looking,

he stuffed it into the trash.

But Lucy saw him and said,
"What are you doing?"

She pulled the card out
of the basket. It had a bit
of frosting on it, and it
was crumpled up.

Lucy looked at the funny-shaped heart. She looked at the hoofmarks and the torn paper. She looked at the squiggle.

She said, "Did you make this, Sparkle?"

Sparkle hung his head.

"For me?"
Sparkle nodded.

Even though Lucy didn't understand what the card said, she understood what it meant.

It meant that Sparkle loved her best of all.

She laughed her great big laugh and said,
"I *love* this! It is *perfect*!"

Sparkle felt like the luckiest unicorn in the world.

To celebrate, he danced on the table and shot rainbow stars out of his horn. There was a star for everyone. Then he ate twenty-ONE cupcakes. They were delicious!

Lucy said, "I made a special card for you, Sparkle!"

Lucy read Sparkle the poem.

It was perfect, too.